I0757490

Strawberries of the Road
From the Hills of West Virginia

Melinda Grisco
Illustrated by Beverly Conner

This book is for:

Abigale Lee

Alexandra Faye

Sylvan

and

Mary

I heard this one from my dad, so it's a tall tale.

Even though he's not really that tall.

The old widow Jenkins lived down there on route 52 on a flat spot of about 2 acres, right across from Pigeon creek in Delbarton. As we all know there just ain't many flat parts along 52 in Delbarton. She wasn't really that old, just felt like it most days. Her life had been hard and full of more challenges than most women face in a lifetime. Yet she carried on. You see, she was a window ever since the big cave in at the old Nagatuck coal mine.

The morning of the cave in was rainy and cold. The workers were glad to be going in, but somehow each one felt a bit uneasy that day. Thirty-seven miners went in that morning—none ever came out. This left a lot of families with no dads, grandpas, uncles, or big brothers. It was a terrible, sad thing. A lot of families had a rough, hard time making ends meet and caring for their own. Food was scarce, money and goods almost didn't exist, and all the neighbors and friends shared what little they had.

The widow Jenkins was left with five children to care for. Five hungry, growing faster, than you can shake a stick at young 'uns. She had a big vegetable garden. She grew lots of greens, 'maters, and rhubarb. She grew some root vegetables like carrots, taters and onions. That was good for the growing months. They ate the food 'bout as fast as it grew.

Once in a while, she and her oldest child were able to shoot a coon, a squirrel or a rabbit for the meat. Sometimes they ate a wild turkey or a rattlesnake. There was no money for bullets for the gun, so they used a slingshot made from a stick, and rocks for ammo. She knew how to make snare traps; they sometimes caught rabbits that way. There were fish in the creek across the road, not as many as there used to be—so many of the people were fishing that the fish were slowly disappearing. The Jenkins family knew how to forage the woods for berries, mushrooms, greens, and lots of their medicine. Why, if they hadn't had medicine from the woods, there would have been none. There was a remedy for everything they needed, from stomachaches to infections, and even cures for fleas on the dog. It was available at the pharmacy in the forest.

The widow did some sewing and washing for folks but barely made enough to buy the kids anything. Why if hadn't been for Jimmy, the old shoemaker none of her kids would have had any shoes. He made the oldest child a pair of shoes every winter and the shoes got passed down. By the time the youngest got a pair they were pretty worn out. The widow had only one pair for herself that she managed to patch together every winter. In the summer they all went barefoot. It's just what folks did, plus all the shoes they had lasted longer that way.

She made the kids clothes out of cloth sacks and rags. It was the best she could do. She would buy the flour sacks, when she could afford the flour, in those bright colorful sacks they made during those times. Ya see the flour makin' people realized how many folks were making clothes out of their sacks and started making them appealing, with little colorful designs on them. She was an excellent seamstress; her mama had taught her, and lord knows she got a lot of practice.

The Jenkinses got their firewood from the hills around them. They went and picked up coal by the railroad tracks. It was the coal that fell off Mr. Peabody's coal train as it left the hills. Most of the coal mined in the hills went to other parts of the country. The Jenkinses had a big ol drafty house; it was hard to heat with the found coal and wood. The old place was not in the best shape, but they were all together, and the roof didn't leak.

GA 34
BLEW•1

One morning the widow Jenkins was at the creek washing clothes with her two youngest children, Sylvan and 'Lizbeth. A big fancy blue truck drove by; the license plate was from a different state. They were some uppity ups that thought they were better than other folks. Those fancy blue truck people pitched their garbage out the window down the hill by the creek.

One of the things in the garbage was a big bushel basket of rotten strawberries.

Well the widow got so mad-hot about this! What in tar-nation could those baloney heads be thinking? What nerve to just pitch your darn trash over the bank into the creek! She ran up the hill to the road yelling and screaming at the fancy blue truck people. All she saw was a buncha' dust and the back end of their vehicle, with that out of state plate on the back.

After choking and coughing on all that dust she went back down to the creek and found her children picking up the trash, including the basket of ol' mostly rotten, mushy smelly strawberries. "Looky here, Mama," Sylvan said, "We got some strawberries to eat!"

"Aw no sugar bear." She began, but paused and had a deep thought, maybe those berries could be put to good use. "Ok, pick 'em up" she said, "we can't eat these, but we can do something else."

The next day she took all those rotten berries and dug some holes in her garden and planted them. When she started to plant them she realized just how many there were! Well you can bet there were over a hundred berries, and some of them had already started to germinate into buds. In a few weeks they had almost all sprouted and started to grow. Now strawberry plants come back every year, and the longer they grow—the more berries come off of 'em.

The next year, the widow and the children all had plenty of berries to eat during the growing time. There were even enough strawberries for the widow to put up a several dozen jars of jam, for the winter. The year after that, there was more than they could eat! So the widow was able to put up twice as many jars of strawberry jam, enough for the whole winter, and a lot left over to boot! She sold the leftover jars and bought a bunch of chickens. She made some strawberry rhubarb pies (they were the best pies in Mingo county!). The next year, why, there were so many berries she made enough jam to sell, and got enough money to buy more chickens and two goats. After that they had enough eggs to eat and even many to sell. The same year they had milk from the goat plus the eggs and the jam-she also made cheese from the goat milk. During these years, she still had her vegetable garden, and now even enough money for ammo in daddy's old gun. This made hunting easier and put more meat on the family table.

JAM
4 SALE

Why, the next year there was enough to get another goat! All those kids got new shoes! For the first time ever the widow even got new shoes. The kids also got winter coats.

The family was rich. They had shoes, clothes, plenty to eat, and a big ol' drafty house. Most importantly, they had each other.

About the Author/Illustrator

Melinda Grisco—Author, raconteur, professional yarn spinner.

After raising her family, she went back to school to earn her Bachelor of Arts degree in Health and Wellness from Antioch Midwest in Yellow Spring, Ohio. Now she continues to travel the globe to collect stories. She lives with her cat, Louisa, in Cincinnati, Ohio.

Beverly Conner—Artist Illustrator.

Beverly has a Bachelor of Fine Arts degree from Wright State University in Dayton, Ohio. After working as an airbrush artist for twenty years, Beverly continues to fulfill her passion for drawing and painting, as well as most crafts and cross stitching. She resides in Xenia, Ohio as an Independent Provider and cares for her youngest daughter at home. Her oldest daughter lives close by and also shares in her passion for cross stitch.